This book belongs to:

First published by Walker Books Ltd.,
87 Vauxhall Walk, London SE11 5HJ

Copyright © 2002 by Lucy Cousins
Lucy Cousins font copyright © 2002 by Lucy Cousins

Based on the audiovisual series Maisy, a King Rollo Films production for
Universal Pictures International Visual Programming. Original script by Andrew Brenner.
Illustrated in the style of Lucy Cousins by King Rollo Films Ltd.

Maisy™. Maisy is a registered trademark of Walker Books Ltd., London.

First U.S. edition 2002

The Library of Congress has cataloged the hardcover edition as follows:

Cousins, Lucy.
Maisy cleans up / Lucy Cousins. —1st U.S. ed.
p. cm.
Summary: Maisy the mouse and her friend Charley clean her
house together and then treat themselves to cupcakes.
ISBN 978-0-7636-1711-0 (hardcover)
[1. Cleanliness—Fiction. 2. Mice—Fiction. 3. Friendship—Fiction.] I. Title.
PZ7.C83175 Mad 2002
[E]—dc21      2001035479

ISBN 978-0-7636-1712-7 (paperback)

09 10 11 12 13 14 SWT 20 19 18 17 16 15

Printed in Dongguan, Guangdong, China

This book was typeset in Lucy Cousins.
The illustrations were done in gouache.

Candlewick Press
99 Dover Street
Somerville, Massachusetts 02144

visit us at www.candlewick.com

# Maisy Cleans Up

## Lucy Cousins

CANDLEWICK PRESS

Maisy is cleaning her house today.

Ding-dong!

Someone is at the door. Who could it be?

It's Charley!

He's come for a visit.

He can help
Maisy clean!

Charley smells something delicious in the kitchen. He's hungry.

Oh, look — cupcakes!

But the floor
is still wet.
Charley has to wait
until it's dry.

While he's waiting, Charley puts the toys away.

Maisy vacuums the living room.

Then Charley washes the windows from the inside . . .

and Maisy washes them from the outside.

That looks better!

At last the kitchen floor is dry.

Now Maisy and Charley can have some cupcakes.

Hooray!

Good job, Maisy.
Good job, Charley.
Treats! Yum, yum!

Lucy Cousins is one of today's most acclaimed author-illustrators of children's books. Her unique titles instantly engage babies, toddlers, and preschoolers with their childlike simplicity and bright colors. And the winsome exploits of characters like Maisy reflect the adventures that young children have every day.

Lucy admits that illustration comes more easily to her than writing, which tends to work around the drawings. "I draw by heart," she says. "I think of what children would like by going back to my own childlike instincts! And what instincts! Lucy Cousins now has more than thirteen million books in print, from cloth and picture books to irresistible pull-the-tab and lift-the-flap books.